Angus&Robertson
An imprint of HarperCollins*Publishers,* Australia

First published in Australia by William Collins Pty Ltd in 1975
First published in paperback in 1979
Reprinted in 1981, 1984, 1985, 1987, 1988
This Bluegum paperback edition published in 1991
Reprinted in 1993, 1994, 1996, 1997
by HarperCollins*Publishers* Pty Limited
ACN 009 913 517
A member of the HarperCollins*Publishers* (Australia) Pty Limited Group

HarperCollins*Publishers*
25 Ryde Road, Pymble, Sydney, NSW 2073, Australia
31 View Road, Glenfield, Auckland 10, New Zealand
77-85 Fulham Palace Road, London W6 8JB, United Kingdom
Hazelton Lanes, 55 Avenue Road, Suite 2900, Toronto, Ontario M5R 3L2
and 1995 Markham Road, Scarborough, Ontario M1B 5M8, Canada
10 East 53rd Street, New York NY 10032, USA

ISBN 0 207 17433 4.

Typeset by Filmset Pty Ltd, Brisbane
Printed in Hong Kong

14 13 12 11   97 98 99

The
Rainbow
Serpent

Written and illustrated by
DICK ROUGHSEY

 Angus&Robertson
An imprint of HarperCollins*Publishers*

Far off in Dreamtime there were only people, no animals or birds;
no trees or bushes; no hills or mountains. The country was all flat.

Goorialla, the great Rainbow Serpent, stirred and set off to look for his own tribe. He travelled across Australia from south to north.

He reached Cape York where he stopped and made a big red mountain called Narabullgan. He listened on the wind and heard only voices speaking strange languages. 'This is not my country, the people here speak a different tongue. I must look further for my own people.'

Goorialla left Narabullgan and his huge body made a deep gorge where
he came down. He travelled north, stopping every evening to listen
on the wind for his own people. He travelled for many days,
and his tracks made the creeks and the rivers as he journeyed north.

Travelling north from Narabullgan, Goorialla made two more mountains.
One of them, Naradunga, was long and made of granite;
the other which had sharp peaks and five caves, was called Gormungan.

His next resting place was at Fairview where he made a lily lagoon called Minalinka. Goorialla turned his great body round and round but the ground was too hard to make it deep.

One day he heard singing on the wind. He heard, '*Ahrrr, AHRRR, AHRRR.*'
'Those are my people singing,' said Goorialla.
'They are holding a big Bora.'
He travelled north with the singing coming louder and louder.

At the meeting place of the two rivers Goorialla found his own people:
they were dancing and singing. He crawled up quietly
and lay in hiding to watch them. He watched for a long time,
then he came out and was welcomed by his people.

He told them, 'You men are not dancing properly and you are not dressed properly. Watch me and I will show you the correct way.' Goorialla showed the men how to fit a lump of beeswax on the back of their heads and use feathers to make a rayed headdress.

He dressed them with pandanus armbands
and placed white bones through their noses.
Then he taught them to dance,
and they copied him until they were tired.

A big storm was gathering—

so all the people built humpies for shelter.

Two young men, the Bil-bil or Rainbow Lorikeet brothers,
came running in looking for shelter, but no one had room.
They asked their grandmother, the Star woman, but she said,
'I have too many dogs—I can't help you boys.'

The Bil-bil boys went to Goorialla and found him snoring in his humpy.
When the boys called out he yawned and said, 'I have no room for you.'
The rain came heavier and the boys ran all about the camp
looking for shelter, but no one would help them.

The boys went back to Goorialla and called out that the rain was heavy.
Goorialla said, 'All right, you wait, I will make my humpy bigger.'
He opened his mouth wide, right up to the roof, and said,
'All right, you can come in now.'

The Bil-bil brothers ran into Goorialla's mouth and he swallowed them.
Then he began worrying about what his people would do
when they found the boys were missing. He decided to travel north
to Bora-bunaru, the only great natural mountain in the land.

Next morning the people asked each other who had given shelter to
the Bil-bil boys. They found the boys were gone and saw the tracks
of Goorialla and knew he had swallowed them.
The men took spears and followed after Goorialla.

Goorialla travelled towards distant Bora-bunaru,
the mighty mountain which towered far up into the sky.
When he reached the cliffs around its base Goorialla crawled up them.
He coiled up for a sleep with the Bil-bil boys inside him.

The people followed Goorialla to the steep base of Bora-bunaru.
The men tried to climb the cliffs: Emu, Turkey, Brolga, Tortoise,
Possum, Barramundi; they all tried but kept falling down again.

Two Wangoo, or Tree Goanna brothers, came along.
Gooranji, the Emu, said to them, 'We cannot climb this steep mountain.'
The Wangoo said, 'We will climb up to rescue the Bil-bil boys.'
They each made a knife from quartz and began to climb the mountain.

The Wangoo brothers climbed for days and nights
and on reaching the top found Goorialla fast asleep and snoring.
They crept up to him and the older brother said,
'We will cut him open; you start down there and I will start here.'

They cut until they reached the Bil-bil boys, who had changed
into beautiful parrots with all the colours of the Rainbow Serpent.
The Wangoo said, 'You can come out, you are now Rainbow Lorikeets
with wings and can fly away.' The Bil-bil birds flew away.

The Wangoo brothers ran down the mountain. Goorialla snored on
until a cold wind blew through his empty stomach and woke him.
He said, 'Something is wrong with me.'
And looked about and saw where he had been cut and his dinner stolen.

Goorialla became angry and worked himself into a great rage.
He began to thresh about in fury, his long red tongue flashing
like lightning, and the great mountain shook and thundered
as Goorialla tore it apart in his anger.

He hurled parts of the mountain all over the country,
to form the hills and mountains of today. All the people were terrified
of the thunder on the mountain as Goorialla knocked it to pieces.

Some of them were killed by flying stones. Others ran away to hide,
turning themselves into all the kinds of animals, birds,
insects and plant life that live in the country today.

That is how it all happened back in Dreamtime.
When Goorialla's anger was spent there was only a small hill
remaining of the great mountain Bora-bunaru. He went down
and disappeared into the sea, where he remains to this day.

Now the remaining people have to look after all the animals,
all the living things which were men and women in the beginning
but who were too afraid of old Goorialla to remain as people.
The shooting star racing across the sky at night is the eye of Goorialla
—watching everybody.